the Packet of gods

and other stories

Gunapala Dharmasiri

Story Bridge Books
2015

Dedicated to Laura Markowitz

TABLE OF CONTENTS

Chalks

He was a very small fellow. He used to bring us milk in the early mornings. One morning, after leaving the bottle in the pantry as usual, he came to me. He was feeling a bit shy. He had never spoken to me earlier.

He said, "I want a piece of chalk."

I asked, "Why do you want chalk?"

"I want."

"Why? What for?"

"I want it. Can you bring one for me?" He knew that I was a teacher.

"Why do you want chalks? Tell me. If you tell me that, I will bring you chalks."

"Hmm…hmm…to work sums."

"I see, you want to do sums. Are they very difficult?"

"Yes…"

"Really?"

"No…not so difficult if I have chalks."

"How many pieces of chalk do you want?"

"One piece."

"What will you give me in return?"

"What do you want?"

"Anything."

"Hmm…I will bring you guava fruits. They are very tasty. There are two kinds. One kind is not good. I will bring you the good one. They are very small."

"Where do you find them?"

"There…over there," pointing the hand, "where those cows graze. Don't you know?"

"Right. I will bring you chalks today. You come tomorrow morning."

He vanished.

By the time I arrived at the school, I had forgotten the whole episode. Next morning, he was at my door.

"The chalk."

"So sorry. I forgot to bring it. I will bring it today. You come tomorrow. Here, did you bring those guava fruits?"

"No. I will give them to you when you give me chalks. Also, remember, I want white chalks."

"How white?"

He raised the bottle of milk: "Like this."

"Shall I bring you some small pieces?"

"No. I don't want small pieces. I want a long one like this."

He found it difficult to choose a finger. He noted that his small fingers would not do justice to the pieces of chalk. He meant an unbroken piece of chalk.

"Shall I bring you colored chalks instead of white?"

"No. I want white chalks."

"Why don't you like colored chalks?"

"Because…I want white chalks."

He went.

For two days I went on consistently forgetting chalks. Both the times I saw how even such a small fellow can have such big hopes and tolerate so coolly the anguish of seeing them crash.

On the second morning I promised to definitely bring chalk. It was a strong promise. Then I asked him casually, "How many pieces of chalk do you want?"

"I want four."

"Oh, that won't do. The other day you asked me only for one. Because I promised you one, now you say four. That is not good."

"Alright. Then one is enough. But it should be white, long and also unbroken."

I saw a grin of satisfaction when I promised.

Unfortunately, for some reason, I could not go to school that day. The following morning he came directly to me and asked for chalks. He was beaming with joy. He was smiling. It was white, white as milk, and white as chalk, I mean really white chalk. There was a twinkle in his eyes, probably a ray of hope.

I told him that I could not go to school the previous day. I told him why and was about to make a very, very strong promise…

The whole world changed. He was crying. He raised his hand to wipe his tears. A packet fell from under his clothes where he had kept it hidden. It burst open. Small guava fruits started rolling on the ground, some to the right, some to the left. They had been plucked some days back, I noted.

I went to my room and thought "The world would be a heaven if we had chalks. The only thing is that we don't have chalks. I mean really white chalks."

The Mystery of Esala Perahera

Esala Perahera is a very big procession that takes place once a year in Kandy. Its origin can be traced back to ancient days. So, it has a deep historical significance. It is valued for its artistic beauty and historicity. The procession winds it way at night for several days. The final night witnesses the procession in its full, culminating grandeur. It is attended by thousands of spectators.

There is a raging controversy with regard to the last day of last year's Esala Perahera. That day, a peculiar thing happened. It is still incredible to many. Yet, none except a very few really believes it, though many people say many kinds of things about it.

What happened was that although the Perahera really took place, on that last day no one came to see it. All the people had somehow come to believe that the day-before-the-last was the actual last day of the Perahera. Therefore, no one came to see the really last one. Usually it takes place in the very middle of the night. Therefore, even the neighboring folk did not come because they were in deep sleep. Most of the people who lived along the streets had heard the sound of the Perahera. But they had thought that they were dreaming because they had seen it regularly over the last few days and had vivid memories of it. So they simply dismissed it and no one came out to see it. When tom-tom beaters and dancers told those at home that they were going for Perahera, their relatives took it for a joke. Some ignored it because they were so convinced that they had seen it for the last day the day before. So, no one came to see it.

But there was the Perahera. It went through the streets and ended as usual.

The general public says that the Perahera did not really take place that day. But there is a mass of evidence against this view. All the dancers and tom-tom beaters swear that they participated in the procession. Each morning after Perahera the road must be cleared of elephant dung (about a hundred elephants participate). The morning after this particular Perahera people found elephant dung on the road. Most people were shocked to see it because elephant dung was taken as the strongest evidence that Perahera had really taken place the previous night. Though peoples' memories can be discounted, this presence of elephant dung cannot be so easily discounted. Such heaps of dung cannot be made artificially. Further, there is no need to do such a thing on the part of any. Therefore, some believe that the Perahera really took place.

Then they asked: "How can all the people be ignorant of the Perahera?"

In fact there had been a wild rumor that was responsible for their ignorance. The believers in Perahera say it was the most effective rumor in the history of the island.

It is said to have been the most beautiful Perahera ever staged. The participants say that they performed their parts so well. The absence of spectators had not affected their performances because, in any case, they have been given hereditary lands by ancient kings for their Perahera service. Though there be spectators or no spectators they have to play their role. They say they were able to do it better that day because they had enough space to dance and move around as there were no spectators. Also, they could concentrate exclusively on dancing. So, they say that day the Perahera was extraordinarily beautiful.

But, as to its beauty, some say that without spectators, one cannot speak of Perahera being beautiful or not. Against this, many aestheticians state that a thing can be beautiful even though no one sees it. On the other hand, dancers had seen each other dancing well.

Some lament, saying that people really lost something because they were not fortunate enough to see the Perahera that day. Others say that the Perahera was the real loser because it lost the spectators. Still others say that both were losers. But particularly in this case, both cannot be losers. Logically it cannot be so. When there are only two parties, only one loses.

Still, the controversy centers mainly around the question of whether Perahera really took place that day or not. There is no way of settling this question. Memories are known to be fallible. The elephant dung heaps made a strong case until the middle of the following day of the Perahera. They remained so until the mid-day. Municipal scavengers did not come to clean them up because they, too, did not think of this Perahera. After mid-day many arthritis patients who came to see this scene carried away lumps of dung (there is a belief among some Sinhalese people that elephant dung cures arthritis). Thus disappeared the elephant dung—the only strong evidence.

To scoop out the available evidence I approached several of those arthritis patients. Some of them said that memories are not reliable, particularly theirs. Others said that those days they were severely suffering from arthritis and therefore were so concerned about their disease that they had forgotten the day they collected elephant dung.

Monotony

The sage stood looking at the stream.

The stream flowed. It followed a bend and came upon a small and sharp elevation at which the water dribbled on to a slab of stone. After a long time the slab thinned and disappeared. It left no mark. Now the water fell directly on the soil making there a small pool-like thing.

The sage stood gazing at the stream. It flowed to eternity. After the eternity, the stream dried.

Little by little the soil filled the small chasm. The accumulation of the soil went on. And there came up a small mound.

"Why this mound at this place, not at any other?" the sage wondered. He knew the answer but did not like to entertain it.

The mound started to become larger and larger. One small grain of dust upon another, another upon another and likewise the process went on for an eon. Now in front of the sage there stood a huge mountain.

The sage stood looking at it.

The mountain lasted for an eternity. After the eternity it started eroding. First it started in a small way and later went on a grand scale. The mountain became smaller and smaller and disappeared completely.

There stood the level ground.

The sage stood looking at it.

There were small plants on it. Tiny insects perambulated around the plants. The sage stood fascinated.

One of the plants, unexpectedly for the sage, changed its tiny course of existence and started to become big. It grew for an eon and became a colossal tree. For the first part of the succeeding eon it went on dying.

The sage stood looking at it.

Again came the level ground, which lasted for another eternity.

After the end of the eternity the sage saw water droplets being formed in a fountain. It overflowed, and started a stream. It became bigger and bigger and a large river stood in front of the sage.

It flowed and flowed. The sage went on looking at it.

It flowed to eternity.

One day several people came to the river-bank and stayed there for some time looking at the river. For days they came there in the evenings. One day, one of them spoke and told the sage, "The world is monotonous."

The sage replied, "No. There is much variety."

That day they went for good, saying that they were so bored.

The sage was dumbfounded.

He went on waiting.

Prediction

It was a hot day. I was coming from the hostel going somewhere. Every time I go from the hostel I invariably cross a railway track. There is an intersection of it near our hostel.

That day the hotness was particular. I saw an old man sitting on the track. He was looking up, at the sky, probably at the sun. I could not understand why he was looking at the sky on such a day, which was so hot. On such days we usually despise the sky. I thought that he was trying to read some future happening in terms of something that was up there. Usually one reads some future with the help of the stars. Every fool understands that there are no stars in the sky on such hot days. He might have been trying to read the future with the help of the sun. But what hellish thing can one predict by the sun, I wondered. The only thing one can predict by such a glaring hot sun is that very soon one day the world is going to be burnt up in a universal conflagration. And he must be trying to fix that date, I thought.

But my thoughts took another turn when I noticed that he was looking down on the earth. Later he started inspecting his feet. He was wearing shoes that were very old. This behavior put me in a dilemma. My former conjecture could not reconcile this new behavior with the old. "What can you think or surmise by your feet or shoes?"

My thoughts were interrupted when he noticed me staring at him. He started.

"Sir, the whole thing is about my shoes; rather, their soles. The soles are wearing off. Though I was looking up at the sky, the sky was not responsible for all this. Now I understand that it was the earth that was responsible for it. The earth has been revolving too much on my soles, so the soles started wearing off. They are worn off enough. Within another few days they will disappear for good. After that, believe me, the earth will start revolving right on my flesh!"

The Packet
of Gods

It was a packet, like a cigarette packet (Its resemblance to a cigarette packet will be made clearer in the sequel.). It was in the middle of the sky. It just hung in the air. It had two openings through the flaps, one up and one down. There lived ten gods in the packet. They stayed huddled together. There was very little space and they could not sit or lie down. They had to stay standing up. It was necessitated by the circumstances. Thus, they all had to stand upright, tucked together. So they felt warm against one another.

Above them was the world of Brahmas. They had enough space and they were more powerful than the gods because they were the creators. They were the ones who had created this packet of gods. They had done it for the fun of it. The world of the Brahmas was of cylindrical shape and it was extremely big. It stood above the packet of gods, which supplied enough fun for the Brahmas who, when they wanted to have some form of entertainment, opened the packet and peeped into it to view the bundle inside. Then all the Brahmas laughed. It was quite interesting.

The gods felt quite happy with what they had. But they had one limitation. They could not move as they wished. Curiously enough they felt as if they moved everywhere. Yet it was a very dreamy kind of movement and was in fact an illusion. However, they could make one real movement occasionally. It was a boon granted to them by the Brahmas. So sometimes a god comes up by opening the upper flap, perambulates the packet and enters back. This was the greatest possible adventure they could dream of and perform. They became really proud and had a sense of achievement after this adventure. In other times they stood huddled together. Surprisingly, they thought they could do everything. They did not know that their one and only possible adventure was a boon of the Brahmas, granted out of sympathy. They imagined that they did many things and felt that they were really doing them, while in fact they were subject to a grand illusion. (However, the difference between the fact and illusion does not matter very much here).

As they stood so close to one another sometimes one's face would touch another's. It was difficult to keep the faces from touching because they stood close as if they were embracing one another. However, when they were perspiring they did not very much like the idea of being so close together, particularly because the smell was nauseating.

The Brahmas had a time of fun with this packet. After some time they started to feel bored with the gods. So the Brahmas took the gods out of the packet and smoked them, one by one, like cigarettes.

The Death of an Idealist

He was a convinced idealist, in the extreme sense, nearing the status of a solipsist.

He ardently believed that the world exists only in so far as he perceived it, and proved it.

"One can never be sure that things exist when one is not perceiving them. How can one ever be sure of an unperceived existence of objects? This table exists only when I see it. If I want to verify whether it exists in my absence I should have to come back to it. It is only then that it springs to life."

Once he met a philosopher who put forward some sundry arguments against his theory. He immediately started advancing an invisible argument. He argued that we may be dreaming. In dreams we see things as existing in space and time. So, all these experiences may be dreams. We are dreaming. In dreams we see things and people.

"So are you and this table dreams," the idealist said.

The philosopher was silenced for good.

He became an absolutely convinced idealist.

He said that the whole world existed in his mind. He created things, as it were. Not voluntarily, but as in dreams. They come so. Why? It cannot be explained. Everything cannot be explained, and need not. Why do dreams behave as they do? So you have to stop somewhere.

He maintained that he was responsible for this whole world. The world existed only for him. But he was a kind fellow and so was worried about the sufferings of his people. It was true that his people were phantoms, but even then "it" was suffering.

Sometimes he got angry. He was the sole owner of the world. When he wanted to do things as he desired, at times, the phantoms obstructed him. Then he became uneasy.

Once he addressed me as "phantom" and said that he was satisfied with me because I was a good phantom. He asked me to obey him. I obeyed him. It was interesting.

He was disgusted with his phantoms. Their behavior was horrible; unruly. They had no morals. In many instances these phantoms stood in his way. But they need not have and should not have. He was the only "man" in the world. So, he had to maintain his rights painfully. For example, to get rations he had to stand in the queue. He resented this. He could have forced his way through, and that would be absolutely justified because he was the justifier. But "some phantoms are mighty," he said, "and therefore it is advisable to wait there."

Because of these reasons he resented his world so much. He wished that he did not have this world.

Until his death I associated with him very closely. He summoned me to him when he was on his deathbed. He told me, "It is only to you that I am going to tell this secret. You are going to die, because I am going to die. My death logically implies your death and that of all the others. I feel pity for the phantoms. However unruly, they were severely interesting. If not for them my life would have been terribly boring. But, now all of them are going to die. It is true that they are phantoms. Nevertheless, 'it' is death. To see even phantoms die is something that I cannot bear."

I was frightened. I thought that he must be telling the truth. I believed him completely because I could never argue against him. His arguments were "invisible," particularly the one from "dreaming." I could not disprove him, I believed, because only he was true. So I strongly held that I was one of his innumerable phantoms. For the first time in my life I felt death approaching me.

He went on: "Now the whole world is approaching death. I have no meaning in the world after my death precisely because the world has no meaning without me."

From the last words he mumbled discreetly I could gather that he was much worried about the fact that there would be no one to cremate him after his death.

An Attempt to Be a Vacuum

One can say there is absolutely no reason why I should write this story. But I strongly feel that all of you should know this, because it is something you should know. And I also feel that because most of us are unaware of what I am going to say, much of the time is wasted in living. This story is all that is left with me now, and as I tell this to you I will be emptying the only burden I am carrying for the last time. After telling this to you I can feel myself a vacuum in the proper sense of the term. A vacuum, mind you, can work wonders. When you are a vacuum it makes no difference whether you live or die.

At the beginning I was a small son of a mother and a father. After some time I became alone and thenceforth I was to be a vagrant. But one cannot live forever as a vagrant. It means it floats. There should be a firm stand to keep one's feet on. Winds and vagaries of time took me to a station and due to some mysterious reason the station master took a liking for me and asked me to do small odd jobs at the place. It was, of course, a railway station, and in time, I got entangled in the affairs of the trains. When the ticket collector was not there I had to collect tickets and wait until the arrival of another train to collect another group of tickets. When the porters were not there I had to carry goods here and there. The job I liked most was that of the time keeper. It was very interesting. There was a board with a list of train destinations. He had to mark the arrivals of the next trains. When the time keeper was absent I did that work. We used chalks; white. The board was black. Whenever a train came we would erase off its time and mark the next arrival time. There were many trains and we had much work.

One day the time keeper died and I had to do his work for the rest of the day. The station master asked me to continue in the work and after sometime he told me that the authorities had appointed me permanently as the time keeper of that station.

I worked unsparingly and punctiliously. After a little time I could recite by heart the times of train arrivals. With the passage of time those train arrivals intruded into the very make-up of my life itself. For example, when I felt hungry in the morning it was time for the 7:15 train going to X. Near the mid-day when I felt thirsty it was the time for the 11:51 train going to A. and when I felt sleepy after my lunch it meant that the 2:20 train was near. In this way the train timetable became ingrained in my life.

I would never fail to mark the very correct time because the commuters were so concerned about the most correct times, and they became highly satisfied with my work. I was always ready with what they wanted. If a train ran late of the appointed time the commuters would get wild and then I would also join in their heated arguments and various forms of harangue until the train arrived. When the train came and they boarded it I would erase off its time and mark the next arrival. The commuters became so pleased with my work that their association one day honored me by presenting a gold medal (of this medal I have more to say later on).

Days and months passed by and I stood in the very heart of the railway mechanism. My life became a matter of train arrivals. When life assumes an eternal repetition it loses its dynamism and vitality and turns out to be nauseating. That happened to me in exactly that way. There was a sickening feeling throughout and sometimes this feeling would grip me torturously in an attack that was unbearable.

I wanted novelty. Without that, I knew, I would die of that sickness. I tried to find out the ways of novelty. One day I wrongly marked the time of a train arrival. That day, many commuters missed the train. There was a loud commotion in the station. People came and made various sorts of allegations against me. One person said that I had turned bad. The station master advised me to be careful. The incident was lively enough for me. It was sufficient to keep me a few days without my usual sickness. But it returned after a few days. Then I would mark a time wrongly, and it would be followed by a commotion, which would relive me for another few days. The process could be repeated only for a limited period. The commuters got to know that I was doing it purposely. This enraged them. They immediately cried for my dismissal. I was thrown out of the station.

Again I became a vagrant. That is for the second time now. The shock I received at the discharge was enough to sustain me for a few days. Then the vagrant life interested me for another two or three days. Again, I relapsed.

I needed violent changes, I knew. I thought, and that night I derailed a train. I was not caught. But several passengers were wounded and some were critically injured. I visited the scene. I heard people crying. It was painful. I knew that it was I who was responsible for that crying. The only thing was that I could not stand to see a human being sob. It was something I never expected. It came really like a revelation. At that moment, for the first time in my life, I felt a pain throbbing in my heart. That was to continue in me forever. But the sickening feeling I wanted to get rid of was in the belly. It was not as positive as this pain. This pain was more positive. My sickness was more a negative one. The severest moments would come as an onslaught enfeebling me and would disappear after sometime. But this new pain was to continue for eternity. After that I never derailed a train.

Now I have nothing to do. I am left with no alternatives, all the alternatives being exhausted. When I look back I see myself as a piece of abnormality. Those days, when I changed the time of a train's arrival by one or two minutes it led to such a commotion among the commuters as if something really vital had taken place. But in fact, it did not make any significant change to the world order. They wanted to have the times given to them very precisely and methodically. I knew some people traveled daily in the train although they had nothing to do. They just traveled. They liked it. Though they had nothing to do, really, they felt, the trains should run methodically. They loved that monotony and repetition. All the people I knew loved it. They loved it with a mixed feeling of awe and wonder, and worshipped it with humble gratitude.

But I was allergic to this god-like phenomenon. So, I conclude that I am abnormal and have come to this world to disturb the sacred monotony of the universe. The implication I draw is that those who cannot adore this monotony should perish by it. Taking the train to be a symbol of this monotony I have decided to end my life by letting a train run over my whole body. That, I can accomplish by lying on a railway line when a train is about to run over it. There is a train scheduled to come today at 5.30 p.m. Sometimes it gets delayed by about 15 minutes. But this delay is not very important whether I am going to live or die. *

About the medal: I have instructed a friend of mine to keep that medal near my coffin. It was shining like gold at the beginning; later, its color began to fade. Those commuters told me then that it was gold-plated. But now I have my doubts. However, if you come to the funeral you can see it for yourself.

The Stitches of Life

It was difficult to sleep. He was having a severe cold and could not breathe. His nose was blocked. He opened his mouth and slept.

He never argued with life. Life was armed with its inexorable laws of determinism. He could only look at life and wait. The only response he could make was passive.

He simply sat on the bank and looked at the river. It was flowing, flowing to eternity and nullity. The river did not really flow; it gushed. It was full of violent currents and whirlpools. Though it was difficult, he wanted to change its course. But it was absurdly difficult. He was one of those who ventured into the impossible. Further, it was absolutely prohibited even to think so. The river should be allowed to run its premeditated course. The river was sacred.

He started thinking for the first time. In his life, he was first an infant (he could not remember that period) and then a child. After that he could remember becoming a boy and then a student. Very recently, he had become a doctor. He was never a "man." He could never be one. The situation had become rigid now. He had been made a doctor and placed in a niche. He was to stick to that. He felt pity for himself.

He worked in a hospital. He had to wait until all humanity was healed of its ailments. Then only would he be a free man and get an off-hour to go somewhere.

There was a patient who stayed for years in his ward. He felt kindly toward the doctor. Once he kept a portion from his quota of milk and offered it to the doctor. The doctor felt flattered and gulped it. A lump stuck in his throat and later it was to choke him. His colleagues rebuked him: "How could you take milk given by a patient? How would it affect the situation of the other doctors?" He felt annoyed. The nurses and others started muttering words. He felt miserable. He was alone. There were only doctors, patients, nurses and workers, but not a single "man." In a world where there are no men one feels lonely.

He went home and told the parents that he wanted to leave his profession. They asked him what he was going to do afterward. He did not know, he said. He only knew that he did not want to be a doctor. Parents had their say. They said that he was made a doctor by them and they wanted him as a doctor, not as a no-doctor. Status and money mattered in a society where doctors are scarce. He could not resign, he was told. He was absolutely determined in his niche.

In the evening he had to perform an operation on a patient. He cut the patient with a scalpel, took out what was unnecessary in the abdomen and stitched. He saw the used scalpel on the table. He thought that he was related to it by a strong kinship. He felt friendly toward it.

After some days the patient was advised to walk. When the patient walked the stitches creaked.

The doctor felt like vomiting. A ghost from behind shouted: "Vomit, Vomit! Hospitals are made precisely for that." He felt flattered again. It was night when he went to the town. Though he did not know, the pen-light he wore under his shirt was on.

The light streamed out of his multi-colored shirt. He looked like a Vesak lantern.

He went to the river bank and sat. A dragonfly perched on his head. It started ruminating.

Then he vomited some yellowish liquid. It had a putrid smell. Black ants started accumulating around it and began tasting it. Some got immersed in it and died. Others had their bellyfuls and went back to their underground halls, which were eternally dark.

He started to think. There was nothing for him to think about. Everything had been thought for him by others. He felt a blank in his head.

He could only look at the river. It eternally flowed. But it was impossible to go on looking at it forever. It was boring. He wanted to decide. But there was nothing for him to decide. Everything had been already decided. He had simply nothing to do.

He felt light. He flew into the river. The river gnashed and ferociously carried him away. No one knows to where.

The Dog's-Eye View of the World

According to its color, the world can be divided into two: black and white. There are borderline cases, no doubt. But those are not very important.

To give a description of man, of which I am somewhat interested, is no easy task. Man is the most complex creature I have ever met with. About all the other creatures you can see something definite and cogent. But a man is a complex conglomeration of several men. Therefore, contradictions are inherent in human nature. As against this, in us there is a homogenous and smooth pattern of behavior. Comparatively, humanity is contradictory while caninity is non-contradictory. That is why man's behavior cannot be predicted. You do not know how a man might turn out to be in a particular situation. Man is an adept in playing in role. For example, he may praise a man in his presence and may do the complete opposite of it in his absence. This role playing makes the human phenomenon all the harder to attempt to understand.

Another incredible feature in man is his ability to balance his body purely on two legs, particularly when some have such massive abdomens. That must be consuming a greater part of their energy and attention.

Roughly speaking, man is something like a machine. (It is only when you go into details that complexities arise.) His life is highly routinized. I was, for some time, much interested in the men called "officers." They typify the exemplary behavior of the routinized man. In the morning they go, and in the evening they come. After some talk and dinner they sleep. Again next day the same routine is followed. People, other than these officers, have their own daily routines. It is extremely difficult to understand what they are really doing. The only explanation I can see is that these routines are how they find means to get the things they want to eat. There are other possible explanations, but none fits so well as this.

There are others who sit on a chair from dawn to dusk and gaze at the world. That is because there are others who find means for them.

In substance, men toil without break. For what? This is the most enigmatic question ever posed. What I feel is that they can do what they do without so much toil.

They are obsessed with unnecessary question and things. They feel that they should have permanent dwellings etc. on a massive scale. In very big houses you may be surprised to find only one or two inhabitants. The buildings are so strong and permanent that one obviously gets the impression that they are going to live for eternity. But ironically, believe my word, they all die. Some die amidst their toil, some after getting tired and some when they are aspiring to toil. After one's death one is paid much attention due to a human being. The amount of attention paid to a person after his death makes one wonder whether he had lived at all. However, so far as they themselves are concerned they do not care so much about death and go on as if it did not exist. The death is purely an accident to them.

Our life paints a different picture. It is very trivial and simple. We have no routines. If there is any, it should be a forced one. We do not accept any such. We live because we have got to live. So, life itself is forced upon us as any other routine is. When we are hungry we go in search of food. Not until then. Our items of food range from absolutely dry bones to marvelous pieces of sandwiches. We come across our food by accident. Food means chance, in other words.

Life is extremely uninteresting for us. We are neither happy nor unhappy. We never toil. We have neither a past nor a future. We always live in the present. There is no anxiety. That is why we can sleep so well. Also, we are never in a hurry. I have heard people say that though we have no work we never walk slowly. They say so because they are so obsessed with reasons. They think that an end justifies all the means and one should be in a hurry only when one has some reason for being so. We are not that type. We never think of reasons. We walk for no reasons. Just, we walk. People seem to get a peculiar satisfaction from finding reasons. When they do not have any, they invent. But should there be reasons for any? This search for reasons lands one in an infinite regress that may lead to an unreasoned reason. But we stop here rather than there. The difference is only quantitative, not qualitative.

We are never obsessed with reasons. We cannot see any. Just, we do things. Things just happen. Ours is a life by accident. That is why we do not feel like owning the world. Men do own the world and feel proud of it. They own; we beg.

Nothing is necessary for us. We see the world as a dynamic flow of accidental events. We passively wait for our turns. Men are obsessed with this phenomenon of necessity. Each and everything is necessary. That is why they risk even their lives for silly and sundry things. We are not worried about permanent residence, etc. It is not relevant.

We balance well because we have four legs. Therefore, our attention and energy are not wasted. When we feel like barking we bark. But we bark in unison. In fact, in most instances there is no reason for barking. In such instances people come out of houses to see "reasons" for our barking. Only after a laborious search do they realize that we bark for no reasons. Then they blame us. Sometimes, we bark at the moon just for the fun of it.

They have thought so much about themselves that they assume themselves to be the only creatures who can think. A man who sees this account of mine might get surprised and say, "How can dogs think like this?" I tell you, that is a typical piece of human thinking.

When we die, we die. We do not grieve. One grieves only when one sees reasons. When there are no reasons, there are no reasons for grief.

It is not at all interesting to look at accidents and wait… wait for death, which means nothing. But it is interesting to see uninteresting things end.

The Clay Heaven

Once upon a time there was a man. He lived in a heaven, a clay heaven. That means his heaven was made out of clay. No one cared to intrude on his heaven because it was cheap clay. He was neither happy nor unhappy. He simply lived, but because he knew the fact that he was living, there was a little bit of anguish. That was all.

After some time, he felt bored. He said that there was no beauty in a clay heaven. So he wanted to add something beautiful into it. And he added some gold to the clay. It looked beautiful, somewhat. And it was thrilling. It was a new experience, at least for him. He was no longer bored. He forgot the anguish. But in its place, now he wondered what trick this new gold might play in his heaven.

The new gold did its work. Clay could not stand with gold for long. If clay is to stick together it should be pure clay. When clay is mixed with a metal, clay begins to crack. He did not know that. He was a fool. And so, clay began to crack. He noted that and said that those cracks were beautiful. No doubt, he was worried about the cracks. But he said that those very cracks themselves constitute "the beautiful." The clay heaven went on cracking and cracking and…and

One day, the whole heaven collapsed on his head.

Puppies

Puppies are puppies everywhere. But it was not so in our hostel. According to our boarding master there were two kinds of puppies: male and female. Males were superior, interesting and therefore to be welcomed. Females were inferior and dangerous because they breed children and therefore troubles. More puppies meant more trouble in terms of food and lodging.

The female dog in our hostel gave birth to several puppies, four in all. They were of various colors. One was absolutely black and another absolutely white. Another was dark black with a brownish tinge and the last was black and white. All were females. The mother was having children for the first time. She delivered them in a deserted house situated above our hostel. They had a quiet time at time at the beginning. After a few days the mother brought one of them down to our hostel. Early one morning she brought it and kept it in the portico and looked proudly at us. It was her achievement. The puppy stayed with us till evening and was studying their varying kinds of play. Thus, all the four were brought down. It was an interesting time for us. We'd had no playmates before, but now we had many.

For our boarding master, this was the first major problem he was ever posed with in his life. He said that he could not keep them in the hostel because puppies invited trouble.

Jamis, our servant, was instructed by the boarding master to take them to a distant place and then drop them there. The following morning, however, we saw the puppies stuck to the nipples of the mother. There was a serene look on her face. At times, she mewed. But we knew that the things had to separate in the evening. She was responsible for not paying the necessary attention to the utilitarian standards of our society. She would have to suffer because she had given birth to something that our boarding master did not like. She loved her children. But the "love" had to conform to the established norms of the human society. That is why the mother would have to part from her children.

In the evening they were gone. There was abject silence in the hostel. No one spoke. None had the courage to do so. We had no feelings; even if we had them they had no place in the world. We read our books and waited for many unexpected things. Until midnight we read, our reading interposed with bickering thoughts. When we were about to sleep one of us spoke.

"They are gone."

We knew that. There was no need to say it. Such things should not be spoken of in public.

However, Jamis had not taken them after all. In the morning when we were going to school we met them some distance away from the hostel. We showed the puppies the way back, but they would not understand. We naturally expected them back in the evening. In the afternoon one of them (the one in black and white) was running along the railway track down by our hostel. She did not look up. She just ran up and down. In broad daylight we could not venture out one step for our boarding master was out there to catch the culprits. She ran up and down until a train decided her destination. We went and buried her in an anonymous place.

In the dusk we could hear the cries of the other puppies penetrating the thin darkness. They were coming, all three of them. The mother did not hear them. We went and brought her to the portico. Then she heard it. She ran and carried one back. It was dark. One of us ran down and salvaged the rest. At night there was a get-together.

Next day, the same problem dawned for our boarding-master. Jamis was given detailed instructions and by the evening they were gone. That night the shrill wails of the mother could be heard in the distance. My roommate said that when children were away the accumulating milk tends to press in the nipples, giving pain. But it was only a biological reason.

From the following day she started frequenting the railway track. She would go up and down and wait. One day she came up with shrieks. We went to see. Her fore-leg was severed at the ankle. A train had done it. A portion was hanging by a piece of flesh. Every time the leg touched the ground she sent up piercing yells. She halted, licked her wound and ran. When she became fed up with crying she started meditating on the wound and tried to understand it. It eluded her canine comprehension.

That very midnight we heard a puppy crying pathetically down on the tracks. We took our flashlights, but there was none to be seen. My roommate told me that it must be the ghost of that dead puppy. It is true that ghosts cannot be seen by flash-light. My roommate knew many things of the world.

A few days later we saw a puppy (the brownish one) back at the hostel. It was a revelation to us, a revelation of the mysteries of nature. No one knew how she had managed to come back; none of us, not even the boarding master.

Now she lives with her mother. She owns a future, which is enigmatic for all of us.

One can see, quite often, the daughter sucking at the mother. When the daughter sucks, the mother's decapitated leg, which she holds up, turns clockwise.

The Man Who Wanted to Live with a Picture

He saw it in an art gallery. It was a picture. It was very beautiful. He fell in love with it.

He started visiting it daily, simply to see it, and he admired it next to his life.

In the first day the picture seemed to be neutral, at least as far as he was concerned. The next day he saw it paying a tiny attention to him. The following day the picture was looking at him. For the first time he saw the picture smiling. His heart was filled and he was overjoyed. That day he went home absolutely satisfied.

Next day, the picture looked decided. Its attention was concentrated on him, or so it seemed to him.

One day he wanted to talk to the picture.

He talked.

The picture did not reply.

Pictures do not talk.

He did not know that, and that day he suffered a lot.

Their love developed rapidly.

Now he wanted to buy the picture. He went to the authorities and talked the matter over. There was a lot of trouble on the way. They said the pictures of that art gallery are not sold. Even if an exception is made it would cost a huge amount. Price was attached to the art gallery rather than to the picture itself. Whatever was sold at that art gallery, if any ever sold, cost much. Its name mattered so much. He did his best to have the picture for himself. But he did not have so much money. He thought of all the possible means. None availed.

He dreamt that the picture was with him. He started thinking of the time when the picture would be with him and how he would then live a picturesque life.

Undaunted, he daily visited his beloved picture. There was the regular smile. It was so regular, but only the smile. He viewed the picture from various angles. He wanted it to behave as he liked. One day he tilted the picture a little to the left and he wanted to it to stay like that. But it slid back to its former position. He got wild.

Again, he pushed it up. But it jerked and fell back to its former position. He got angry and went off. Next day, he wanted it to swing. He gave the momentum, but it soon regained its balance and poise.

The pictures are moved by the laws of natures.

For days he went on visiting his beloved without fail. They smiled, smiled and smiled. One day he saw that the picture was showing him too much admiration. It was smiling too much. That day he felt the picture cheap and wanted to spit at it.

Once, suddenly, he noted that the picture's color was fading. He asked the authorities and they came and saw to it and said that it was due to the cheap paints with which the picture had been executed.

It went on fading and lost its charm. After that he did want to see it look at him, and looked at it from a distance and disappeared.

He was so happy that it never talked with him and never behaved as he wanted. Above all, he was absolutely happy that the gallery did not allow him to buy it.

The color would go on fading and fading and at last only the rough cardboard would remain. It was incredible for him to conceive how he could live with a cardboard.

The Sage and the Tortoise

The sage wondered in silent meditation.

Someone came out of the mud in the nearby pond and stood in front of the sage. It was a tortoise.

The sage opened his eyes and dozed.

The tortoise said, "I have heard you instruct people on how to obtain release. I want release."

The sage asked, "What is the release you want?"

"I want release from my shell."

"Why do you want that release?"

"I know and understand that it is a grave hindrance in my path to happiness. I know it protects me, but it also obstructs."

The sage sermonized: "If you are released from your shell you will perish. You can live and be safe only within the shell. That means your release means your death. It is meaningless to talk of such a kind of release. You can never find it."

The tortoise laughed with delight: "I found release!"

The sage was thunderstruck. "How can that be?"

The tortoise rejoined: "I am released from liberation."

The sage became enlightened.

About the Author

Gunapala Dharmasiri, Ph.D., was Professor of Philosophy at the University at Peradeniya, Sri Lanka, from 1965 until his retirement in 2007. He earned his doctorate from University of Lancaster in England and is the author of many books including *The Buddhist Critique of the Christian Concept of God; Fundamentals of Buddhist Ethics* and the forthcoming *Buddhism and Sex*. He has also translated dozens of Mayahana Buddhist texts from English into his native Sinhalese. Dr. Dharmasiri was founder and organizer of the Bhikkshuni Foundation, which supported the education and higher ordination of Buddhist nuns in Sri Lanka.

Dr. Dharmasiri wrote this collection of short stories in 1967. Several of the stories have appeared in Sinhalese-language publications and in *Hibbert Journal* (Allen and Unwin) and *PRISM International* (British Columbia University).

The author currently lives in Kandy, Sri Lanka. To contact Dr. Dharmasiri, or for more information, email info@ storybridgebooks.com